BIRDIE's LIGHTHOUSE

written by

DEBORAH HOPKINSON

illustrated by

KIMBERLY BULCKEN ROOT

AN ANNE SCHWARTZ BOOK

Atheneum Books for Young Readers

For my own lighthouse family—
Andy, Rebekah, and Dimitri
—D. H.

To Bertie Shanberger, with affection
—K. B. R.

Acknowledgment
Special thanks to Robert Davis of the Shore Village Museum, Rockland, Maine; and Wayne Wheeler, United States Lighthouse Society, San Francisco, California.

Atheneum Books for Young Readers
An imprint of Simon & Schuster Children's Publishing Division
1230 Avenue of the Americas
New York, New York 10020

Book design by Ann Bobco
The text of this book is set in Horley Oldstyle.
The illustrations are rendered in pen-and-ink and watercolor.
Printed in the United States of America
10 9 8 7 6 5 4 3 2 1
Library of Congress Cataloging-in-Publication Data
Hopkinson, Deborah.
Birdie's lighthouse / by Deborah Hopkinson ; illustrated by Kimberly Bulcken Root.
p. cm.
"An Anne Schwartz book."
Summary: The diary of a ten-year-old girl who moves with her family in 1855 from a town on the Maine coast to rugged Turtle Island where her father is to be the lighthouse keeper.
ISBN 0-689-81052-0
[1. Lighthouses—Fiction. 2. Maine—Fiction. 3. Diaries—Fiction.]
I. Root, Kimberly Bulcken, ill. II. Title.
PZ7.H778125Bi 1997
Fic—dc20
94-24097

1855

January 15

My name is Bertha Holland, but most folks call me Birdie. Before Papa went to sea, he gave me this pretty diary for my birthday. My cat, Blueberry, likes it almost as much as I do—but only to sit upon!

I was born ten years ago today, here in our cottage by the sea. Hannah Flowers, the mid-wife, told me the waves roared awful loud that night, right up till I was born. Then they softened and lulled me to sleep. Old Hannah says that means I'm kin to the ocean.

February 4

Today Nate and I climbed the cliffs to watch for Papa's boat. We looked far out, where the lighthouse clings to a patch of black rock called Turtle Island.

I told Nate that when I was little, I believed I could tie one end of a string to my finger, and the other end to Papa's boat, and Papa would never be lost. Nate laughed. We don't have any magic string, but I hope the lighthouse's beam guides Papa home soon.

February 16

This morning it was thick o' fog, and no sign of Papa's boat. Nate and I went to the village to ask if the fishermen had any news. Mr. Willis said not to fret, Papa's a real blue water man and there's no finer sailor in Maine. I want to believe him, but in my heart I know these deep, cold waters are stronger than even Papa.

March 5

Mama sang lullabies to little Janey for a long time tonight, rocking back and forth, back and forth, in the old black chair. Her head was bent down close, but I could see her tears.

Mama says after Papa comes home, she hopes he won't go to sea anymore.

March 20

Papa is back, safe!

April 16

Mama got her wish! Tonight Papa came bursting in with the news—he's been chosen the new lighthouse keeper. It's a great honor, for everyone depends on the light-keeper. With its bright beam, the lighthouse warns boats of dangerous rocks and marks the mouth of our harbor. If the light is dark even one night, a boat could be lost or ship-wrecked.

What will it be like, I wonder, to live on that lonely island all by ourselves?

May 1

I was so sad today. Mama said Blueberry is too old to go to Turtle Island. I had to give him to Cousin Sally. I hugged him one last time and tried not to cry.

Then we loaded our belongings into the dory and set off. Good-bye, Blueberry! Good-bye, everyone!

We were cold and shivering by the time we reached Turtle Island. From the boat, it really did look like a giant black turtle hunched in the sea.

What wild, rough waters! Jagged boulders loomed over us, casting cold, eerie shadows. I remembered a story the fishermen told of a night when the lighthouse went dark, and a grand schooner slammed into these rocks and was lost.

I held my breath, terrified our little boat would be dashed to pieces, too. But Papa steered us through the maze of sharp rocks, and at last we landed safely.

May 5

When I looked out my window this morning, I couldn't keep the tears inside. There's just our bleak little house, the lighthouse tower, and bare, empty rock all around us. At breakfast Mama gave me an extra dollop of syrup on my fritters to make me smile.

Nate is even more unhappy. He'd rather be a fisherman. But at least he gets to help Papa with the light; Mama keeps me busy with lessons and taking care of Janey. Since Janey is walking now, I have to hold her hand all the time. It would be just like her to wander away and topple off a ledge.

May 18

Outside it's dark and foggy. "Smearin' in," the old-timers call it. I feel that way inside, too. I remember a day last spring, when Sally and I found the first buttercups in the meadow. We lay in the soft new grass, tiny golden flowers tickling our ears. I wish I could plant flowers here, but the strong sea winds would blow them away.

June 15

Today Mr. Willis sailed by in the *Sunbeam*. I shouted and waved till my arm hurt.

The air is softer now. I guess spring touches everywhere, even here. The sea is like a shimmering blue meadow, with feather white breakers for wildflowers. We don't have trees, but gulls and terns are nesting on our ledges. And this morning I saw a seal!

I like to climb to the very top of the tower. Somehow, up there I belong to the salty breeze, bright skimming clouds, and clear, deep waters as far as I can see.

July 9

At supper Nate told Papa he wants to work on a fishing boat. Papa would rather Nate stay, to become the assistant keeper. But after a long talk, he said all right. Nate whooped with joy.

Papa will need help now. He isn't sure a girl can do it, but I *know* I can learn to keep the light. I won't let him down.

August 4

My dear brother has left. He'll live in the village with Mr. Willis and work on the *Sunbeam*.

From the top of the tower, I watched the dory till it was out of sight. Nate spotted me and waved. I hope he couldn't see me crying.

August 15

A lightkeeper's day starts early. At sunrise Papa and I climb to the lantern room at the top of the tower. We carefully blow out our fourteen lamps and fill them with whale oil for the night ahead. Then I polish the silvery reflectors that help make the light into a bright beam that boats can see from miles away.

Just at dusk we light each lamp again. Papa has taught me how to trim the wicks at midnight, so the lamps burn steady through the night.

Our lamps take a lot of care, but no matter what, we can't let them go out.

September 11

Papa lets me take the midnight watch now. I like to tiptoe across the rocks to the tower, wrapped in a bright cocoon of stars. *Clang! Clang!* Passing sailors ring their ship's bell, grateful for our light that keeps them safe.

Alone in the tower, I curl up with the old lighthouse logbooks and read about the brave families who lived here before. Last night I read about a time it breezed up so hard the house was almost washed away. The keeper's family had to wait out the storm for days, huddled in the top of the tower.

Papa keeps the logbook for us. Each night he writes, "Light bright and steady. Signed, Nathaniel Holland, Keeper."

October 26

The supply boat came today, with flour, salt pork, potatoes, and cornmeal. And treats, too—fresh apples and maple sugar!

Best of all, we got a letter from Nate. Every morning he sees Blueberry sunning himself in Sally's window. What a lazy cat—I can almost hear him purring! I know Nate and Blueberry are happy now; still, it's hard to be apart.

Nate is coming to visit after his next trip aboard the *Sunbeam*. I can hardly wait.

November 15

This morning we heard the *Sunbeam*'s bell as it sailed up the coast. Mama sighed and was quiet all day. She can't rest easy when someone she loves is at sea.

November 27

It stormed yesterday. Papa stayed up all night to keep the lamps burning. He took sick, and by this morning had a high fever, so I did all the work alone.

Nate should be back soon.

November 30

Today it was coming on to blow, the wind whipping the waves into whitecaps. As I studied the swirling clouds the way Papa taught me, in my head I could hear his warning: "Mares' tails and mackerel sky, never twenty-four hours dry."

I didn't want to worry Mama, but in the lighthouse logbook I wrote: "Lightkeeper sick. Another bad storm coming. Light bright and steady. Signed, Bertha Holland, Keeper's daughter."

December 1

It's a northeaster. Two boats sailed by, racing to get safely into harbor. But where is Nate?

Mama sits by Papa's bed all the time, Janey beside her. I tend the lamps alone, and listen for Nate's bell.

The sea is never still. Sometimes it roars so loud it drowns our voices. Mama says there hasn't been a storm this fierce since the night I was born. She thinks it too dangerous for me to go to the tower again. Yet what else can I do? I'm the lightkeeper now.

December 2

Midnight. Time to check the lamps. I tiptoed by Papa's room. In the lantern glow I saw Mama dozing by the bed, and Janey bundled in a nest of blankets on the rug.

I whispered good-bye, but no one heard.

Outside, the wind screamed and waves pounded the shore. Water came rushing toward me. I put up my hands just as a cold, black wave knocked me down.

My lantern was gone—now I was a little boat, lost in the dark storm. I looked up at the flickering light of the tower ahead. I wanted to turn back. But I kept on, until at last I pulled open the tower door and crawled up the stairs.

I was shivering so, I could barely trim the wicks. In time the lamps stopped smoking and burned steady again. Then I felt so sleepy. . . .

When I woke, it was dark—too dark. The lamps were almost out of oil. I rushed to fill them. Soon the lantern room glowed, and the beam reached out into the darkness like a bright strand of hope. To keep awake, I stood watch.

"Please don't be so angry," I whispered to the ocean.

Toward morning I spied a dark shape in the distance. A boat, struggling in the storm! Could it see my beacon through the thick mist and rain? All I could do was hold my breath and watch, and hope the light shone clear and strong.

I feared the boat would surely crash. At the last moment it veered away from the rocks and slipped by, heading safely into harbor.

Suddenly, above the storm, I heard a familiar sound. *Clang! Clang!*

I knew that bell! I knew that boat!

December 4

The storm is over at last, and the *Sunbeam* is in harbor. I twirled Janey around till she squealed with laughter. Mama says Papa will get better quickly, now that he knows Nate is safe.

December 20

Nate is here! Papa is all well now, and went to fetch him in the dory. Nate said Papa is so proud of me he told everyone in the village how I kept the lamps burning and saved the *Sunbeam*.

Mr. Willis says I'm the bravest lightkeeper in Maine, and Mama thinks it a wonder I wasn't washed away. Well, maybe Old Hannah was right. Maybe I am kin to the ocean.

My birthday is coming soon, and Papa brought me a wonderful surprise—a tiny black kitten! Papa says his new assistant keeper will want some company on these cold winter nights.

1856

January 15

I am eleven today, and have come to the last page of my diary. Papa has promised to bring me a new one next time he goes to the village, so I can write more about my life on Turtle Island.

Blackberry is already getting big. He's a very good kitten, though he does like to chase sea gulls. Most of all, he likes to keep watch in the tower at night, with the light shining bright.

That's what I like best, too.

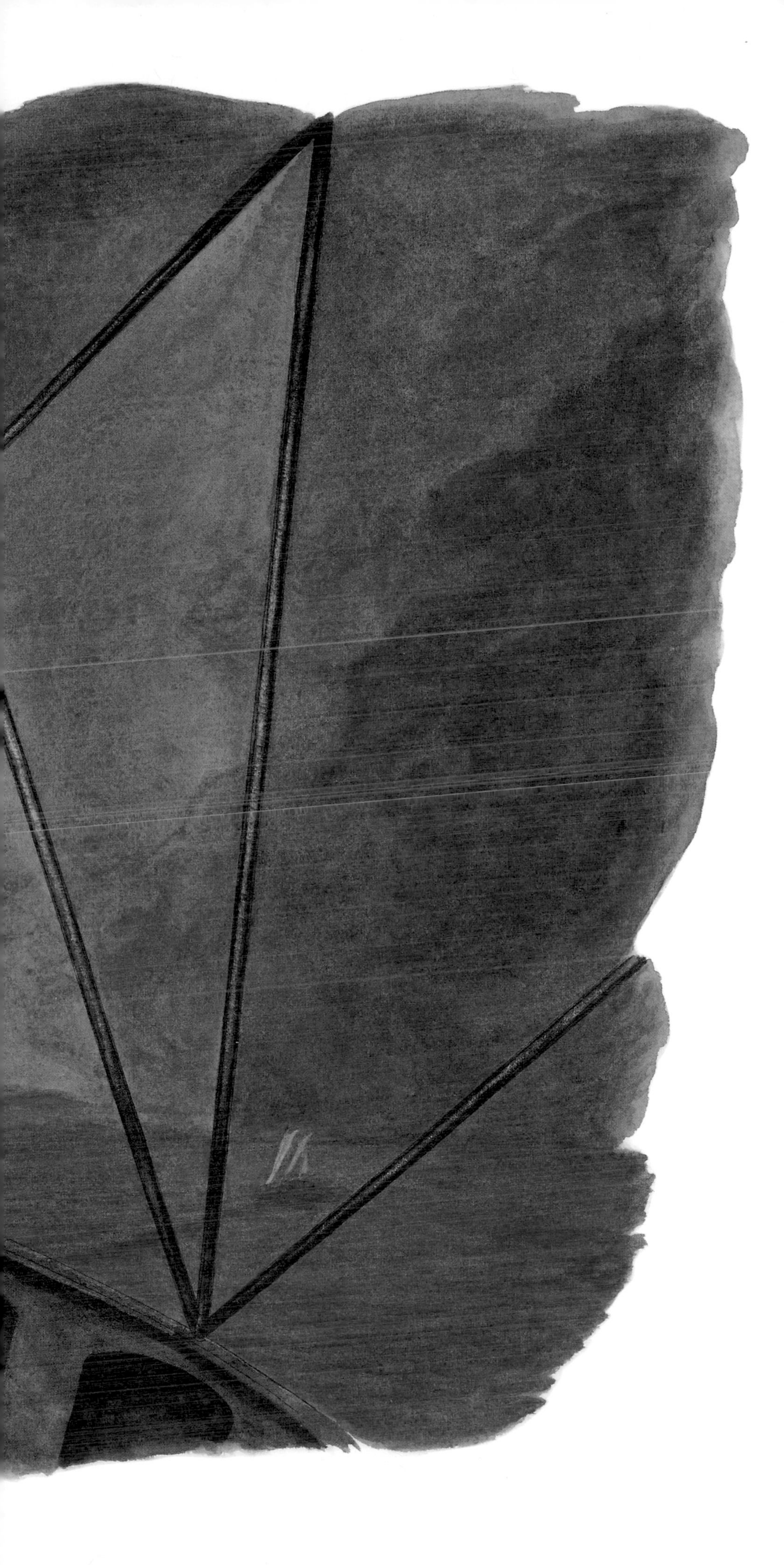

Author's Note

Birdie Holland is not a real person, but her story was inspired by many true-life lighthouse heroines.

In 1838, twenty-two-year-old Grace Darling lived with her family in Longstone Lighthouse off the coast of England. After a shipwreck, Grace and her father performed a daring rescue of nine people who clung to nearby rocks.

In the 1860s, Mrs. Thomas Bray, of Thatcher's Island Lighthouse in Massachusetts, was left alone at the lighthouse with her two little children during a snowstorm. She managed to keep her babies safe—and keep the lamps bright in the island's two lighthouse towers.

Ida Lewis was a famous lightkeeper who tended Lime Rock Light in Newport, Rhode Island, for more than half a century, until her death in 1911. She saved over twenty people from drowning and was so well known that she received a visit from President Ulysses S. Grant.

Perhaps Bertha Holland (whose first name means "shining") is most like another Maine lightkeeper, Abigail Burgess Grant, who lived on an isolated island called Matinicus Rock. In January 1856, when she was seventeen, Abbie kept the island's two towers lit for four stormy weeks while her father was away.

Like Birdie, Abbie grew to love her work. She married another lightkeeper and lived her whole life in lighthouses. Toward the end of her life she wrote, "It has almost seemed to me that the light was part of myself." Perhaps Birdie would say the same.